Once there was a shipshape man
who had everything he needed—
nothing more, nothing less.

Old Robert and the

PHILOMEL BOOKS

AN IMPRINT OF PENGUIN GROUP (USA) INC.

Barbara Joosse

illustrated by Jan Jutte

Sea-Silly Cats

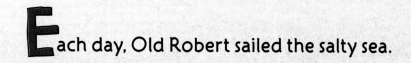

Each day, Old Robert sailed the salty sea.

Each night, he docked his boat.

Old Robert would not sail at night.

There was scarce light.

So he prepared his supper of toast in buttered milk
and counted the regular things in their regular place:

Clean socks

a clock

my ship in the slip at the dock.

One dish

one spoon

a slice of the silver moon.

Old Robert gazed at the moon.

He was silent.

One evening,
there came a sound much like the wind,
whh-whhhh-whhhhhhhhhhhrrr.
But it wasn't the wind.
It was a cat,
dancing.

The cat spun 'round in a pale pink dress
light as a whisper, soft as a secret.

Old Robert began to smile.

Then the cat asked politely, "May I come in?"

Old Robert thought not!
There was no room in the trim little boat
for a cat to live—
and that's that!
And yet . . .

    and yet . . .

        Old Robert said yes . . .

. . . and the cat came in.

Old Robert prepared toast in
buttered milk for two,
then went to bed
and gazed at the moon.
It was bigger.

As he drifted off to sleep,
he counted the regular things
in their regular place:

    Clean socks

    a clock

    my ship in the slip at the dock.

    One dish

    one spoon

    a wedge of the silver moon . . .

       and a cat

       in a wee little hammock.

The next night, as the cat danced 'round,
there came a sound much like a foghorn,
hhhUUUUUUhh.
But it wasn't a foghorn.
It was another cat,
singing.

The cat strummed a ukulele
and sang a story of courage.
He sang the story of love.

Then the cat asked, "May I come in?"

Old Robert thought not!
There was no room in the trim little boat
for *two* cats to live—
and that's that!
And yet . . .
     and yet . . .
          Old Robert said yes . . .

. . . and the cat came in.

Old Robert prepared toast in buttered
milk for three,
then went to bed and gazed
at the moon.
It was bigger still.

As he drifted off to sleep,
Old Robert counted the regular
things in their regular place:

Clean socks

a clock

my ship in the slip at the dock.

One dish

one spoon

a chunk of the silver moon . . .

and two cats

in wee little hammocks.

The next night, as the cats danced and sang,
there came a sound much like the waves,
lap-smack, lap-smack.
But it wasn't the waves.
It was yet another cat,
juggling clackety spoons
and catching them neat
on his ears, nose, cheeks
and tail—*ta-da!*

Old Robert laughed,

    and even before the cat asked

        Old Robert said yes . . .

. . . and the cat came in.
Old Robert prepared toast
in buttered milk for four
and gazed at the moon.
It was filling with gold!

As he drifted off to sleep,
Old Robert counted the regular things in
their regular place:

Clean socks

a clock

my ship in the slip at the dock.

One dish

one spoon

half of the golden moon . . .

and three cats

in wee little hammocks.

The next night, as his darling cats
sang and danced and juggled,
Old Robert clapped for joy.
What a merry din!
Still, the softest sound came through:
mew.

Old Robert didn't wonder
and neither did the cats—
there was one more cat on the dock.

But this cat was just a *cat*.
A scrawny cat
with ears too big
and neck too long
who didn't dance or sing or juggle.
It just sat.
Looking at Old Robert.

Old Robert scooped her up,
this smallest cat
with sea green eyes
who didn't do a single thing.

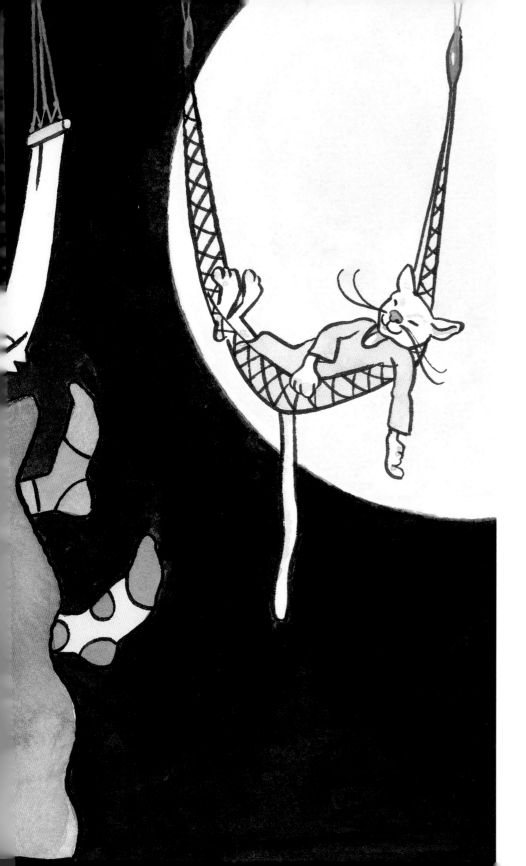

He took her in
and prepared toast in buttered milk
for five.
Afterward, he shook his head.
There wasn't room
for one more hammock . . .

. . . and so Old Robert cradled her
upon his chest.

The moon filled up

then spilled across the sky

and sprinkled down upon the waves

winking at Old Robert—GO!

Old Robert did *not* sail at night.

And yet . . .

and yet . . .

tonight seemed *right*.

And so it was. Old Robert sailed away at night
by the light of the golden moon—
with three cats in wee little hammocks
and one there, upon his chest.